DEDICATION

To my beloved mother
Barbara Lyris Lord
who introduced me to:

The One Who
came to heal the brokenhearted
The One Who
came to set the prisoners free
The One Who sets at liberty
them that are bruised.

I will forever be eternally grateful!!!

FOR CONSCIENCE SAKE

CAROL LORD-PAUL

authorHOUSE®

AuthorHouse™ UK
1663 Liberty Drive
Bloomington, IN 47403 USA
www.authorhouse.co.uk
Phone: 0800.197.4150

Published by AuthorHouse 04/05/2016

ISBN: 978-1-5049-9815-4 (sc)
ISBN: 978-1-5049-9817-8 (e)

CONTENTS

Acknowledgements

To my husband Tony who was my inspiration for 'Anton' a man whose faith is real and raw.

To the rest of my family both immediate and extended who have encouraged me throughout this journey.

To my friends especially Lorraine Johnson, John Wells and Sue Linford who took the time to give me constructive feedback.

Most of all I would like to thank the Lord for all He has done in my life. I pray that He will bless this work and use it as an inspiration in that we would strive as the Apostle Paul said 'to always have a conscience void of offence toward God and toward men'.

PROLOGUE

CHAPTER 1

Year -1998

Place –San Diego, California

She said her name was Gaby.

And that's all Alan could recall as he sat on the floor trembling.

Despite the howling wind outside, sweat steamed down his chest.

Unable to move he only could sit there.

Alone.

In the dark.

And watch.

Calling 911 was not an option.

Gradually, he became aware of light coming into the room, a door opening, hurried footsteps and the sensation that he was a million miles away. It took a moment before Alan realised where he was. Then it dawned on him that he must have been sitting there for hours. The darkness had become daylight.

Jed was shaking him.

'Wh...what's going on? Wh...what happened?' Jed's voice was hysterical as his eyes frantically looked around the room.

Drawing close to the girl lying on the floor Jed put a trembling finger against the side of her neck. There was no pulse.

'She's dead', he said.

Alan's head fell back against the wall, his left hand covering his mouth. His heart began to race. His muscles tensed. Fear swept over him like a tsunami as he remembered the shaking and the white foam.

She was dead.

'Wha...what happened?' Jed repeated.

Alan swallowed, trying to work saliva into his mouth. Aware that Jed was waiting, looking for an explanation he couldn't give.

'I dunno Jed, sh…she just collapsed'. His voice was hoarse.

Alan ran his hand nervously through his shoulder length blonde hair. His eyes darted around the room. It was a mess. The counter cluttered with leftover food, paper plates and empty beer cans. Pills were lying on the coffee table next to two ashtrays filled with cigarette butts. Half-empty glasses were lined up around the bar. Everyone had gone. Alan's head was pounding. How did this happen? Who was she? Questions buzzed around his brain like angry wasps as he vaguely recalled this girl coming on to him at the party. But there were many girls vying for his attention last night, nevertheless, it was this one he woke up to find lying next to him in the bed the early hours of the morning.

Alan put his hands on his forehead 'Sh-she started convulsing and wh-white stuff was coming out of her mouth… I didn't know what to do Jed'.

Alan shook his head in disbelief, 'All I could do was watch'.

Jed was pacing up and down the living room wringing his hands. He shook his head as the situation became clear to him.

'I just knew something like this could happen. She's probably one of Brad's druggie friends'.

His dreadlocks fell forward; his hand brushed it back revealing a face that reflected his anguish, his eyes wide, eyebrows pinched.

'If we call the ambulance, we're ruined'.

He turned and squatted before Alan looking directly into his hazel eyes.

'Come on Al, try and remember'.

Alan drew a breath and met Jed's gaze with tears coming down his face 'I…er I c..came down stairs - just needed to get some black coffee. When I came out here in the living room she was coming down the stairs complaining of a headache. Before I knew what was happening she was taking one of those pills and downing from that bottle,' he pointed to a bottle of vodka on the coffee table. The floor was wet with the spilled liquor, the smell unmistakable.

Realisation like a spear reached Alan's head as he slowly eased himself up. He grabbed hold of the mantelpiece, Jed held him to brace him from falling. This couldn't be happening.

Everything was going so good for him and Jed. They were due to fly out to New York next week. The party was in celebration of their good luck. Labour Under Correct Knowledge is what Dave their boss had called it. Often comparing Alan's work to political cartoonist Garry Trudeau.

'You boys are going places,' he'd said congratulating them on their contract.

And they were going places. All the late nights of sketching and planning had finally paid off. Jed the journalist, he the comic strip artist. They were a team and were going to have their own column in the *New York Times*.

'Alan, we need to stay calm man and … think,' Jed said turning to the girl lying motionless on the floor.

He knelt down and started rummaging through her jacket pockets.

'There's nothing, no ID, not anything, do you know who she even is, who did she come with?'

Alan's head was swimming, remembering people coming and going and didn't notice Jed run up the stairs. He vaguely recalled the room being packed. Everybody looking to have a good time.

He scratched his forehead.

'Her name is Gaby'. Alan shook his head. 'Was Gaby, d-don't know who she is'. He closed his eyes remembering her by the bar eyeing him with her sky blue eyes as she moved slowly to the beat of the music. She was petite and pretty in her denim jacket and mini skirt, with a mass of blonde curly hair underneath her cowboy hat.

Alan turned and slowly staggered towards the body. The room seemed silent.

Where was Jed? Was he even here? The floor reeled as if he were on a ship in a storm.

He rubbed his face partly because it expressed his pain and confusion, mostly because his face was a tangible reality, he could feel it, it was real just as the body lying in front of him was real. Alan's heartbeat quickened and his hands trembled as he stooped down gently turning her over. The girl was limp, her eyes partially open. His hand went to move her hair away from her face, he saw that it was not her natural colour, dark roots were beginning to show. An acrylic necklace with the name Gabriella hung around her neck. Her midriff top revealed a small diamond in her belly button and a small butterfly tattoo.

Something drew Alan back to her eyes. He remembered them rolling back. Now they were staring straight ahead. He felt he was looking at the sky before the sun disappears.

Was that a twitch? Or was it him?

Was that her leg? Could she be alive?

Was he going mad?

'Jed!' Alan's voice came out strangled and hoarse. *Where was he?* He felt he could hardly breathe.

'I'm upstairs' Jed called out 'wanna see if there's anything up here to tell us who she is, a handbag or something.'

Alan, suddenly felt as though he was two people, he saw himself reach for the cushion on the couch, hold it over her face, then put it back. He closed her eyes.

'Found this bag in your room, but there's hardly anything in it.'

Jed was coming down the stairs carrying a small black bag and a pair of cowboy looking boots and hat.

'All it has is a piece of paper with our address on it, a pair of keys and lipstick...not even a mobile phone, no nothing....

He shook his head.

'I just don't get it.'

Alan took a deep breath, one breath at a time, his mind needed to settle on some workable scheme of reality, just one simple pathway he needed to get himself together.

Suddenly with a new resolve, Alan stood up and reached for a cigarette and lighter kept on the mantelpiece. He slowly lit up.

'We're going to have to get rid of the body' he said. 'We'll wait until tonight...not too many people about'. Alan's speech accelerated. 'We'll use your Dodge pickup.' He looked around the room 'We're going to have to put her body somewhere...in one of our suitcases, yeh ...we're gonna have to get our stories straight if the cops come'.

Alan was aware he was talking too loud, too fast, but he couldn't help himself. It was as if he was putting all his pain and guilt into a course of action, into something that he could control.

'Come on and help me get those boots onto her feet' Alan stubbed his cigarette into the overflowing ashtray.

Jed looked at Alan, not too sure what had come over him but too anxious to pay much attention. He put the handbag and hat down and helped Alan put the boots on to her feet.

'I'll tell you what Jed… you go and get a blanket from upstairs and I'll check in the garage to see if we have a big enough suitcase.'

Alan walked through the living room into the kitchen and opened the door to the garage.

Several suitcases were stacked on top of the shelves. He picked the largest one.

CHAPTER 2

The sky was overcast and the humidity rising. There would be a much-needed storm before long Alan thought as Jed drove that night.

They were both tired and exhausted having spent the rest of Saturday clearing up the mess waiting for night to fall to get rid of the body.

'Where are we going?' Jed asked turning south on Rock Springs Road.

'Just drive', Alan urged looking at his watch.

3:00am.

The streets were very quiet. They drove in silence.

Soon they were heading toward Avocado Highway Interstate 15.

Slow drops of rain splashed the windshield.

'Isn't Lake Hodges straight ahead?' Jed asked, his hands holding tight to the steering wheel.

'Yeh, there's the sign', Alan pointed.

'Turn right'.

Alan took a side-glance at Jed as he made a right turn heading south toward Lake Hodges. He was known as' Jed the Dread' back in UCLA, wearing his dreadlocks more as an expression of ethnic pride than one of religious beliefs. His locks were now tied in a pony tail, his jaw set firm, eyes looking straight ahead.

Alan couldn't tell what was going on in his mind. His career, his future, their future. For as long as Alan could remember Jed was a man driven to succeed. He was the first person in his family to climb out of poverty and earn a degree.

They met in their sophomore year in high school when Mr. Ramsees had set the class a project to research 'The Most Frequently Challenged Books Of The 20th Century'. He teamed the two together noticing their talent for persuasive writing. Their friendship developed as they researched John Steinbeck's 'Of Mice and Men' censored for its offensive and racist language. Arguing that Steinbeck's representation of dialogue was far more effective than the use of description got them the highest marks in the class and sealed their friendship. In their senior year Ramsees encouraged them to apply to UCLA where they both worked for *The Daily Bruin*. Alan remembered how relentless Jed was in his studies, especially in their first year. Whilst the freshers were enjoying their first year of freedom Jed would be in his room perfecting his craft...writing.

'The only place where you can find success before work is in the dictionary', he would admonish Alan repeating one of Ramsees favourite quotes.

'Have you read what Jed the Dread said?' was the common question around campus. His articles in the opinion column gained him notoriety.

Alan wound down the window and threw his cigarette out.

How could this have happened?

How would this affect their plans?

He leaned back, his head was throbbing.

A line from a poem suddenly like lightening flashed across his mind.

'The best laid schemes o mice an men...' the words were uttered under his breath.

'Gang aft-agley', Jed finished. He too remembered.

Alan unexpectedly went cold. Jed tightened the grip on the steering wheel.

'Well laid plans go awry'. It was a line from Robert Burn's *'To a Mouse'*.

Startled by this brutal realisation they looked at each other as the same thought simultaneously pierced them both like a dagger.

Would this...could this be the catalyst that destroyed their dream?

Two men lose their dream when a girl dies accidentally.

But we are not two fictitious characters in a book. Alan reasoned. This is not John Steinbeck's *'Of Mice and Men*. This is not some book report they are researching. This is their life...a living nightmare.

'Look Jed...you don't have to do this, you know I...

Jed put his right hand up, interrupting him before he could go any further. His voice was tight.

'We'll talk about this when we get back Al – my head is too mixed up to think straight right now'.

Alan shook his head and took a deep breath. If only he could turn the clocks back, start the day again but there was no comfort in such wishful thinking.

Jed's eyes were intense as he took an exit ramp onto West Bernado Drive onto the gravel road leading back along the river.

'I'll pull in here', he said coming to a dense area covered by trees.

Alan's stomach wrenched inside him as Jed brought his 1998 Dodge Dakota to an abrupt stop.

'Let's just get this over with quick.' Jed's voice was flat as he opened the glove compartment and took out the flashlight.

Alan climbed out the pickup truck and listened. He could hear the sigh of the lake, the sleepy whisper of the black cottonwood leaves, the crickets. Nothing more. He went to the back of the pickup truck and lifted up the tailgate cover. The suitcase was underneath the blanket. Suddenly Alan's heart was in his throat; the darkness around him felt heavy and threatening.

'Should we leave her in the suitcase or take her out?' Alan's voice trembled as he handed Jed the flashlight.

'Let's just take her body out,' Jed replied.

Alan didn't hear him as the first real wind kicked in drowning out Jed's voice.

He could see through Jed's determined expression that he wasn't about to repeat himself. Jed just shone the flashlight on the suitcase while Alan opened the lid. They both stared. The girl was lying in a foetal position as though asleep.

Their eyes met. Without a word Jed handed the flashlight back to Alan. He scooped the girl up in his arms and slung her over his shoulder.

Stumbling over the gravel Alan cursed his hands for shaking as he led the short distance to the lake with the flashlight.

A far rush of wind sounded and a gust drove through the tops of the trees like waves.

CHAPTER 3

Sunday night had become Monday morning. Alan woke up slowly, savouring the sweet state between dreaming and reality. However, gradually, steadily, the real world returned, nudging him when he didn't want to be nudged. He sat up, regrouping about the reality of his situation. He was a criminal. He had watched a girl die or had he killed her, he didn't know? Whichever, he was responsible for her death.

Images of her body tossed in the lake kept replaying in his mind. He was angry at the whole situation, at himself. He went downstairs. The television was on. Jed was in the studio typing away at the computer. Alan could hear him muttering to himself, as he edited and clarified with a vengeance. He was annoyed.

It was mid Sunday morning when they got back yesterday. They hardly spoke to each other the rest of the day. Later on in the evening Jed told Alan that he just wanted to get some sleep, to put the day behind him. He didn't want to discuss anything.

Maybe he couldn't.

Alan came into the studio and leaned on his easel.

'Jed, we need to talk.'

Jed looked up from his computer. He looked tired, his eyes were blood shot.

'Okay Alan'. He folded his arms across his chest and leaned back on his chair.

Alan needed to talk. Jed neither encouraged or discouraged him. He sat back on the chair quiet and receptive.

'The cops are eventually going to be coming around Jed. We need to get our stories straight'.

Jed straightened up and leaned forward. His spoke with frustration.

'What story Alan? There is no story'. Jed turned back to the computer clicked file and exit. 'Listen, we don't know who the girl is or was, there were way too many people for us to remember every face. Her death was a tragic accident.'

'Yeh Jed, but she must have come with someone', Alan sat on his stool by his easel.

'I'm sure Brad's got something to do with this' Jed sounded irritated – anyway where is this cousin of yours?'

Alan sighed as he got off the stool. 'I'm going to get some coffee, you want one?'

Jed nodded. 'There's still some in the percolator'.

I know how you feel about Brad, but Jed you just don't understand', Alan said heading toward the kitchen, 'I feel a sense of responsibility for him, he has no other family'.

'That's just it, Alan, I do understand', Jed was frustrated as he turned the computer off.

'We all go through rough times, okay he's lost his family but he's been staying with us for over a year now and has done nothing except get himself into all kinds of mess. He's nearly thirty. What's he going to do when we go to New York huh?'

'C'mon man, we don't need to argue right now', Alan said handing Jed his cup of coffee.

They'd covered this ground too many times before.

An unexpected knock interrupted them. They looked at each other. Silence hung in the air. 'It's probably Brad, he's always forgetting his key'. Alan walked toward the door.

A gust of wind hit him as he opened the door.

It was Connie their neighbour from the apartment opposite. Suddenly Alan felt embarrassed as he realised that he hadn't showered let alone shaved. His eyes still felt swollen.

'Hi Connie,' Alan tried to sound casual. 'Bit windy for you to be out.'

'I know Alan, just wanted to pop over and give you and Jed a present. Really going to miss you guys when you go. Sorry I couldn't make it to your party last night, but you know its not actually my thing'.

She gave Alan a hug as she handed him a wrapped box.

'Thanks,' Alan was deeply touched.

'I better go, the wind's really kicking up, by the way you need to take that bike in.'

Puzzled, Alan looked further outside the door and saw a bike leaning against the wall.

Funny he hadn't noticed it before, but then again he and Jed had used the back door from the garage.

'Alan, come quick listen to this' Jed yelled.

Alan closed the door. Jed was standing in front of the television. There was a picture of a girl with dark brown hair and blue eyes on the screen behind the newsreader.

Underneath was the caption – 14 year old epileptic daughter of Sheriff missing.

Alan looked hard, the girl looked younger, but it was the girl.

Gabriella Collins known as Gaby.

She was the daughter of a Sheriff and only fourteen!

Alan felt sick. The wrapped box slipped unnoticed and forgotten from his hand onto the floor.

The camera was focused on the parents. The mother was crying. The father's face etched with pain. The news report said that she was last seen riding her bike late Friday afternoon.
Jed looked at Alan.

'What if it wasn't drugs, what if ….?'

A loud knock at the front door suddenly made them both jump.

'I'll go get it' Jed went to answer the door when he came back his face looked drained.

'Al it's the Deputy Sheriff and he's asking for you', he whispered.

Alan's heart dropped. They couldn't have found the body already.

He went to the door. Standing outside was a tall well built man. The small nameplate above his badge read Steve Ellis.

'Alan Moses?'

'Er yes'.

'Mr. Moses, I'm Steve Ellis County Sheriff's Deputy, I'm afraid I have some bad news concerning a Bradley Randolph Jacob'.

Alan relaxed. What's he done now he thought?

'Unfortunately a tree fell and hit his car, he was killed instantly'.

CHAPTER 4

Year: 2008
Place: London, England

Randy knew there was no going back.

The decision was made. It was time Anton knew the truth. Would Anton understand? Would he be able to put himself in his position and imagine the dilemma he had faced? Could he appreciate the fact that there had been no time to weigh or seek other alternatives?

Making his way down the red and gold carpeted aisle to the back of the church sanctuary Randy sensed his shoulders slump, but straightened up to nod, shake hands and smile as he went through the foyer and out the oak double doors. A gust of wind hit him going down the church steps. Speckles of snow were drifting as if the clouds weren't sure whether to keep back or give way. Exactly how I feel Randy thought wiping the cold from his face and pulling his coat closer, his mind colliding with conflicting emotions. Several cars filled the parking lot as people exited the building in a steady stream.

Heading towards his car, someone yelled, 'See ya Randy, looks as though we could have a White Christmas!'

'Yeh' Randy agreed. Everyone was so friendly. He waved as he put the key in the car door.

Despite the cold weather, Randy's hands were sweating as he settled himself into the driving seat. He felt claustrophobic and loosened the knot in his tie.

When he first started attending the church, Randy remembered looking for the hype, for the phonies, even the con but he never found it. Turning the key in the ignition his eyes once again were drawn to the name engraved in front of the building. New Life.

How appropriate, he thought. To think, six months ago 'Jesus' was just a name used whenever he got angry. A dead figure on the cross his Aunt Kate wore around her neck.

However, there was nothing dead about this place. It was *Alive.* He experienced it in the heartfelt songs that were sang and the stirring messages in Pastor McKenzie's preaching. The sign in the front of the church declared… *'In Him was Life and That*

Life was the Light of Men' and he felt it. It was like a beacon of truth easing into a world that knew nothing but lies and deceit.

The Truth Shall Set You Free' is what Pastor McKenzie had entitled his message that morning and it was those words that were replaying in his ears as he pulled out the church parking lot heading Southeast.

The Truth.

Set Free.

Anton deserved to know the truth about his past. Fear had kept that door closed, now faith was pushing it open, assuring him that this was the only way to move forward in his Christian journey.

Randy's hands were tight on the steering wheel, his adrenaline pumping as he drove the twenty minute journey towards Vauxhall. He turned right, pulling into a side street opposite Vauxhall Station where Sunday parking was free to encourage Christmas shoppers. Turning the ignition off, he leaned his head back against the car seat.

Positioning his hands on the steering wheel, ten o'clock and two o'clock. *'God'*, he silently prayed, *'Help me to face the truth, to face the consequences of what I am about to do.'* Heart pounding he sat quietly. All of a sudden he remembered something Pastor McKenzie said that morning, 'God doesn't bring you so far to leave you, He doesn't teach you to swim to let you drown'. God was with him. Refreshed by hope, he got out, slammed the car door shut and with calm deliberation crossed the road cutting through the pedestrian tunnel at the station.

'Hey mate you got a light?'

Unsteady on his feet a disheveled looking man wearing a heavy rumpled overcoat came toward Randy. A cigarette dangling from his mouth was nearly half hidden by his unkempt beard.

Randy shook his head as he passed him. The man approached someone else.

It had been three months and Randy still felt a sense of pride in knowing that he had kicked the habit.

As he walked down the Kennington High Street heavy drops of snow began falling. Randy felt a chill go through his body and wished he'd brought his scarf as he passed Christmas shoppers all bundled up in their scarves and gloves.

Anton had suggested they meet at Mama's Home Cooking, a family-run, Caribbean restaurant, situated on the High Street, a place favoured by local cricket fans. It was located on the corner.

Walking into the restaurant from the bitter cold Randy found the décor appealing as a warm summer breeze with its bold and vivid colours.

Soft reggae music playing in the background added a warm ambience to the place. Magnificent murals of great West Indian cricketing legends such as Brian Lara and Courtney Walsh adorned the walls.

An attractive young girl, of about eighteen, with shoulder length braids came towards him. *The owner's granddaughter,* Randy presumed. She smiled warmly.

His eyes were drawn to the name on the badge. He caught his breath.

'Gaby'.

'Gaby' a name that bought guilt and shame and had sent him running all those years ago.

Images of her face frozen in time came up before him.

There was no escaping what had to be done.

'Hi, can I help you?' she asked.

'I've not made a reservation,' Randy explained, 'but do you have a table for two?'

'No problem' she replied, 'Tends not to be too busy on a Sunday afternoon, people come later on in the evening.'

She turned ushering him through the archway, towards the back of the restaurant. They passed a lounge where three men were sitting around a bar.

Sky News was on. They appeared to be engaged in a lively discussion.

'People were voting who had never even voted before', said one of the men.

'Yeh mon, people were looking for a change'... another interjected.

'I tink de people expectin a lot from de man yu know,' said the oldest looking of the trio.

Randy presumed they were talking about the newly elected President Barack Obama. Everything was changing. If he decided to go back, he would be going back to a different America. Bill Clinton was going through impeachment proceedings when he arrived in England on that wet and windy December morning. *Had it really been ten years since he got off the train at Kings Cross?*

'Is this okay?'

The young girl's voice interrupted his thoughts as she pointed to a booth in a secluded corner.

Randy glanced around the room.

It was near a large window. He could see the Oval Cricket ground from a distance.

'This is just fine,' he said easing himself into the seat and eyeing the mural scenes on the wall.

When his gaze returned to the waitress, he realised she was looking at him. Randy found her warm smile discomforting.

'Can I get you anything to drink before you order?'

Randy's stomach was feeling too nervous to think about food or drink nevertheless he picked up the menu from the table. He knew very little about Caribbean cuisine. His only exposure was the curry goat eaten at the Notting Hill Carnival when he and Sophia went there last year. Aunt Kate had always insisted that he learn more about the 'Caribbean' side of his family, but he really had no interest until recently.

Through two generations of the mixing of the races, with his blonde hair and hazel eyes, there was nothing that could be seen of Randy's West Indian roots. Nonetheless he did notice that the fruit juices were made from fresh fruit. Then there was the 'Café Caribbean' a warm winter cocktail. Just what he needed on a cold day like this.

'Ok I'll try the Café Caribbean, er without the rum please', he said standing taking his coat off and laying it over the chair.

She smiled and headed back through the archway.

Randy sat down and leaned his back against the chair. He closed his eyes and loosened his tie again as fear threatened to strangle him.

The truth had hit him like a bullet square in the chest. He had to be honest with himself. Not only had he confessed to God but he also had to be honest with Anton and trust God with the consequences. Truth always has consequences. He took a deep breath as he glanced at his watch. Two o'clock. *Anton should be arriving any moment now.*

Was this what it was like for a baby to take its first steps?

'Here we are.'

The waitress was back carrying a small tray with an Irish coffee glass, topped with whipped cream.

She set the glass down and smiled.

'Mama likes us to ask our customers to put their glasses at the edge of the table if you would like another drink so we don't have to disturb you by reaching over to fill your glass.'

'Sure, that's not a problem.' Randy smiled politely.

She was looking at him with a curious expression on her face.

'You look just like' she paused 'that guy who forgot who he was in that film… Bourne Identity, what was his name? oh yeh, Matt…yeh Matt Damon'.

She laughed. 'I guess people tell you that all the time'.

With his chiselled good looks and recently cropped hair cut people were often making that comparison. However, Randy was not in the mood for conversation, so he simply nodded.

'Are you American?' she continued, the tray now held at her side.

'Yeh from California.'

Suddenly Randy saw Anton's salt and pepper hair across the room, he was waving.

Randy breathed a sigh of relief. *Thank God.*

'Ah, there's my friend,' he said beckoning to Anton.

He did not mean to sound so curt but Randy knew his weakness and he had been trying to shake off the 'Randy Andy' image.

His mind momentarily flew to Sophia, the beautiful Italian who had shared his life for the past five years. He was not in love with her but their relationship had been comfortable.

Sophia, top model in her day, until an accident had left her slightly paralysed, did not ask any questions about his past. She had an Art Gallery where Randy would do on the spot caricatures at her exhibitions. 'Perfect ice breaker' she would say. Women humoured and flattered by his keen eye were forever inviting him to dinner parties, promotions, conferences. One thing always led to another. Upon reflection he could see being with so many women was his way of escape, a mask - a bit like the caricatures he drew 'You can be anything you want to be' he would tell the women as he got his creative juices flowing. It was all a false impression, a façade, just like his 'Randy Andy' image.

He now knew it was because something inside him was empty. He remembered how hurt Sophia was when he moved out.

'Randee, I don't understand,' she'd cried with mascara running down her cheeks, 'what is it about this God of yours, where was He when I had my accident?' His discussions with her made it clear that he was alone in his newfound beliefs. The Bible, *'Basic Instructions Before Leaving Earth'* as Anton called it, was no longer a book of myths and fables. He found that he no longer questioned. The more he heard the more he believed.

Her views of God were scientific and dismissive while his hunger to learn more increased. She could not understand why he would want to spend time with 'those boring Christian people studying a book full of superstitions'.

He eventually found a bedsit near the church. He continued to pray that one day she would come to understand and forgive him.

Now he had this young girl in front of him eyeing him with interest. She was very pretty with her flawless ebony skin and her eyes like her smile sparkled. She would make a good sketch.

Nevertheless, Anton's arrival was perfect timing. Her face flushed her embarrassment.

'We should be ready to order in about fifteen minutes.'

She nodded, lowering her head-walking pass Anton as he came towards Randy.

CHAPTER 5

Randy had a lot of respect for Anton. He was a warm, effervescent man with a direct manner who had a way of working in a conversation about God with such ease that it was like he was talking about his best friend. Having grown up on the toughest streets of Brixton, Anton was not someone whose faith had been formed through a life of detachment, it was real and raw.

He left home at fifteen, when his mom's new boyfriend moved in. Delroy was a drunk, violent man, possessive of his mother and heavy with his fists. Anton took to the streets when his mother told him she was tired of trying to keep the peace between them. Friends took him in for a while, 'sofa surfing' is how Anton described his nomadic lifestyle to Randy. His life however, took a dramatic turn when one of his friends invited him to New Life Tabernacle. 'I felt obligated to go' Anton explained to Randy, 'after all I was sleeping on their couch. My friend John came from a Christian family. It was the first time that I had seen faith in action. God was the backbone of everything they did.

They prayed with me, encouraged me to finish school and gave me hope for my future'. That was thirty years ago. Anton was now a Social Worker and serving as part of the Pastoral team at New Life Tabernacle. He and Randy's friendship had developed over the months since Anton had invited him to the church.

Randy looked upon Anton as a father figure.

He stretched out his hand to shake Anton's hand.

'Thanks for agreeing to meet up Anton; I know how Sundays are important to you and your family.'

'Yes, Jessica really wanted to come' Anton said taking off his coat and settling himself in the seat opposite to Randy, 'but... she could see you needed to talk.'

'She's a lovely girl and very perceptive' Randy observed.

Anton nodded, as if he expected nothing less of his only offspring.

'They've gone to Denise's parents for dinner. Jess loves her grandma's cooking'.

Randy took a sip of his Café Caribbean. It felt warm in his stomach. Has a year really gone he reflected since that day when

Anton's ten year old daughter Jessica had pulled her Daddy towards his stall at Covent Garden begging him for her picture to be sketched?

Anton put on his glasses as he looked over the menu. He then took his glasses off and directed his gaze towards Randy.

'Okay, what's the problem son, something is obviously bothering you?'

Typical Anton, straight to the point. So much for casual conversation.

Randy felt a muscle jerk in his cheek as he wrestled with the voice in his head. The self doubts began to stir but he fought it down, the self-hatred, struggling pride and fear. All the things that had sent him running so long ago. He couldn't allow them to stop him again. Then he heard the words again, comforting words- *'The Truth Shall Set You Free'.*

Randy leaned across the table. His heart was racing but he was determined. This was the only way to move forward.

'I've been living a lie'...*Bad start.* He cleared his throat, 'My name is not Randy Jacob and I've been living under a false identity for...for ten years'. His well rehearsed words fled.

'Come on, you're joking' Anton laughed then stopped. Randy's face was pale and distraught, his anguish apparent.

'No, it's true. My real name is Alan Moses. Randy Jacob is... was my cousin'.

Anton's face registered disbelief; eyebrows raised in shock.

He shifted in his seat and leaned forward 'Wh-what are you saying...?'

Randy's hands were shaking as he took a sip from his glass.

The words came pouring out like water.

Ten years ago, I was living in California. My partner Jed and I had just got a job with the *New York Times*. The cartoon editor had seen our work and wanted us to do all their cartoons for them. We even got a call from Gary Trudeau. We were so excited. Everything was going good'. Randy took another breath. 'We decided to throw a party. People were coming and going. Drugs were everywhere...girls were everywhere, dressed in the shortest of skirts, all looking to have a good time. I was really enjoying the attention'. Randy paused; he couldn't even begin to think what was going on in Anton's head. However, Anton's concerned expression compelled Randy to continue his story.

'There was this girl there; she looked about seventeen or so. Don't know who invited her…it doesn't matter now'. Randy's eyes moved from Anton's direct gaze to the mural scene above Anton's head and his voice lowered. 'She said her name was Gaby and she just kept coming on to me Anton, she just kept coming on to me'.

Anton shook his head and waved his hand.

'It's okay son, just take your time'.

His tone was encouraging. It invited confidence without demanding it.

Randy sighed heavily. He spoke slowly his words more precise.

'It was about four in the morning when I woke up. She was lying next to me'.

Anton look puzzled.

'Wh…who was lying next to you?'

'Gaby'.

Anton slowly nodded his head, taking a deep breath he folded his hands on the table.

'Everything is a bit hazy now, I remember waking up and going downstairs to the living room. Everyone seemed to have gone. The room looked a mess. There were some white pills on the table and half a bottle of vodka. Then she was there again, complaining of a headache. Before I knew it she was popping a pill in her mouth and downing it with the vodka. Next thing I know she's on the floor struggling for breath. Her lips were turning blue, white vomit coming from her mouth. I panicked Anton, I was too scared to call 911'.

Randy shook his head and covered his eyes.

Anton was silent, waiting for him to continue.

Randy took another deep breath.

'How could I have been so callous?' Randy swallowed the acid taste in his mouth. I was more concerned about my future, my career than the fact she could be dying'.

'What happened next?' Anton's question reflected the concern on his face. His eyes reflected something that was hard to identify. It was as if he had been waiting for this moment of truth or so Randy felt.
Randy fought the urge to pick up the menu and shield his eyes from Anton's direct gaze.

A tear trickled down his cheek.

'Jed was in his room and didn't hear anything. It wasn't until the morning...' Randy's voice drifted off and he took another breath blinking back the memory of all the commotion playing in his head as if it were yesterday.

'It was Jed who felt her pulse, and said that she was dead. Can't remember whose idea it was to just dump her body in the lake. We didn't even know who she was. It wasn't until the next day that we saw on the news that she was the daughter of a sheriff and only fourteen years old!'

Anton closed his eyes, Randy wasn't sure if he was praying or just taking time to digest this incredible story.

Randy continued rushing his words which had became a broken whisper.

'We were so scared because of who she was, we had to get away to think. Then...then my cousin Brad got killed in a car accident. I had to identify the body. Everything was happening so fast. Then we had this Hurricane Isis'.

Anton nodded his head remembering the catastrophic event.

'Fourteen people were killed. As fate would have it, Jed was in that number'. Randy's eyes welled up again as he remembered his friend Jed, a man whose future stretched out before him like a promise golden with hope.

Randy took another deep sigh, as he looked out the window at the people going about their normal lives. 'The apartment was wrecked. Sure people think I'm dead'.

'What about family?' Anton queried.

'My dad abandoned us when I was born, my mom couldn't cope so I was raised by my aunt and uncle. They live in New York, but we lost contact way before I became a cartoonist. My uncle didn't want me to be an artist. Had an argument when I left for UCLA, was hoping to patch things up when Jed and I got the contract. I couldn't wait for him to see our column…that was fifteen years ago. Haven't seen em since. I know this all sounds crazy Anton, too neat to be believable'. Randy shrugged his shoulders and looked out the window, staring at nothing in particular.

'I came to England using Brad's passport, thinking I could start a brand new life with a new name. Getting work where I could, use people to get what I wanted,' the memory of Sophia's bewildered tears still fresh in his mind. 'Life was okay I was getting by or so I thought until I met you and you invited me to church'.

The room fell silent despite the gentle calypso music now playing in the background. A clock ticked loudly.

Anton appeared lost in thought as he looked pensively out the window.

'Well', Anton paused for what seemed an eternity, then cleared his throat. 'I'm glad you told me son, I've always felt there was something you were wrestling with…but knew you would tell me in His time'.

Randy shook his head as Anton continued.

'Jesus came to set the captive free Randy, and that's what He wants to do in your life, to set you free, God forgives you Randy, the hardest battle is you forgiving yourself'.

Randy nodded, Anton was right. He was surprised to remember something his Aunt Kate used to say – 'confession is good for the soul', despite the remorse, he felt a sense of peace settle over him. He rubbed his forehead. 'In the last six months my life has been changing…. ever since I've been coming to the church. It seems as if the messages that Pastor McKenzie preaches has a direct bearing on my life, like he's been reading my mail. He's made God seem so…so touchable…so personable. I don't understand it myself but I've felt a love that was deeper than the pit that I found myself in. I'm thirty three but for the past ten years I've felt like a little lost boy … just wandering around in a desert'. Randy shook his head and smiled faintly,' Now I feel that I've found my way home. I thought I could be free from my past, I tried to ignore it - thought that I could bury it, but I now know that its held me as a prisoner. I have been in a prison of my own for the past ten years'.

Anton's gaze held a look of understanding and warmth. He nodded.

'Are you ready for me to take your order now?' The waitress' voice startled them both.

Had fifteen minutes passed already?

'You know you must try the jerk chicken' Anton remarked adjusting his glasses, 'it's said to be the Caribbean answer to the American barbecue'.

Randy smiled. His stomach rumbled, surprised he realised he was hungry.

Taking Randy's menu Anton quickly glanced over it. He ordered the jerk chicken with rice, plantain and salad for them both.

The young girl took the menu, smiled shyly and left.

Randy ran his hand through his tousled blonde hair. A relief had settled over him like a cool shower. He knew what he had to do.

Anton's look said he knew too. Randy's eyes shimmered pain and hope mixing in a pool of tears. 'I'll be going back to the States'.

Anton closed his eyes and slowly nodded his head. 'He certainly has a strange way of moving'.

Randy looked puzzled.

'Who-whaddya mean?'

'God has a strange way of moving', Anton slowly repeated.

Randy shook his head, 'I don't understand'.

"Well, your name certainly suits you" He paused. 'Alan Mo..ses' The name was said slowly, thoughtfully.

'Do you know the story of Moses?' Anton asked.

Randy raised his eyebrows, 'Only what I saw in the movies with Charlton Heston. I remember the scene when he parted The Red Sea'.

Anton leaned forward, and looked at Randy. 'The scriptures tell us that a good name is better to be chosen than many riches and I don't think it's a mere coincidence that your last name is Moses'. Anton's smile was knowing. Strong. His gaze radiating with faith.

He spoke with an assurance. 'Your life draws many parallels to the life of Moses. Moses was adopted, and like you he caused someone's death, hid their body and ran away. But God had a purpose for him, just as He has a purpose for you. Read it in the book of Exodus. Have faith in His plan Randy...er Alan, no matter how dismal it may look. As He was with Moses He'll be with you, as He parted the Red Sea for Moses He'll part it for you in your life'.

Despite the sharp truth in his tone, Anton's words were as sweet as honey. He stretched out and clasped Randy's hand.

'I'll be praying for you son'.

Anton paused as if trying to find the right words, his eyebrows narrowed. 'You have now come out from behind that...that fig leaf of guilt and shame'.

Randy nodded his head, Anton's metaphorical expression made it abundantly clear. He understood Adam and Eve's need to clothe themselves in fig leaves. Shame and guilt does that–it makes you want to hide.

'There's no telling what God can do with a life that is fully surrendered to Him Randy', Anton assured him.

Randy's prison of secrets had crumbled. He did not know what the future held but he knew Who was holding it.

YOUR DECISION

At some stress filled point in our lives which of us has not wondered, what it would be like to walk out of one life and begin another. Is it really possible to leave your troubles behind?

You, the reader are probably wondering why stop the story there. What is going to happen to Randy/Alan? What will his future be? Will his newfound faith give him the courage to face the consequences of his actions? Will he end up in prison?

What makes Randy's story so unique is not the fact that he could have gotten away with the crime, but he could not live with his conscience after being confronted with the gospel of Jesus Christ.

A newspaper reported in 2004 that Dan R. Leach who had gotten away with murdering Ashley Nicole Wilson confessed to police after seeing, 'The Passion of the Christ' and talking with a friend. A coroner had ruled her death by hanging a suicide. Similarly Johnny Olson of Norway confessed to two arson attacks and Turner Lee Bingham confessed to several robberies. Each credit the film prompting them to come forward confessing to crimes they could have gotten away with.

Back in 1970 Katherine Power, a student at Brandeis University in Boston, was the leader of radical National Student Strike

Force. She and several others planned to raise money to buy arms for the Black Panthers by robbing a bank. Kathy agreed to drive the getaway car. To make a long story short, the robbery got botched up and a patrolman was killed by one of Kathy's accomplices. Kathy was immediately listed as armed and dangerous on the FBI's most wanted list.

In the late 1970's Kathy moved to Oregon, changed her name, settled down, started a business, bought a home, got married, started a family, and became active in her community.

She had every reason to be at peace, but at age forty-four she was desperately tired, tormented by guilt, and chronically depressed. So finally she did the only thing she felt she could to end her agony. In September 1993 she turned herself into the Boston police and confessed. She explained, "I am now learning to live with openness and truth rather than shame and hiddeness'.

Do you have an inner voice telling you what is right and what is wrong? What about people who commit horrific crimes against humanity? Is there an inner voice crying out, disturbing their peace and sleep?

The Bible has much to say about our conscience. There is no word for 'conscience' in the Old Testament Hebrew, but it is illustrated often. Joseph's brother certainly felt the sting of their conscience, when they first came to Egypt to purchase food.

Joseph's identity was concealed, he tested his brothers, accusing them of being spies and stealing corn. We read their response in Genesis 42:21. They said to each other, 'We are guilty concerning our brother, in that we saw the anguish of his soul, when he besought us, and we would not hear; therefore is this distress come upon us'. Their treatment in Egypt awakened thoughts in their hearts that had lain dormant for two decades. They did not know they were in the presence of their brother. Joseph wasn't dead, he was alive, and so was their conscience.

Oswald Chambers in 'My Utmost for His Highest' said, 'Conscience is that ability within Me that attaches itself to the highest standard I know, and then continually reminds me of what the standard demands that I do. It is the eye of the soul which looks out either toward God or toward what we regard as the highest standard. This explain why conscience is different in different people. If I am in the habit of continually holding God's standard in front of me, my conscience will always direct me to God's perfect Law and indicate what I should do. The questions is, will I obey? I have to make effort to keep my conscience so sensitive that I can live without any offence to anyone.

God as our Creator has created us as moral beings. As such, God has equipped every human being with a 'built in' moral conscience. We see evidence of this in Romans 2:14-15. 'For when the Gentiles, which have not the law, do by nature the things contained in the law, these, having not the law, are a law unto themselves. 15. Which shew the work of the law written in their hearts, their conscience also bearing witness, and their thoughts the mean while excusing one another.' The Law was given to the Jews, but the Gentiles had the work of the Law, written in their hearts. Their conscience bore witness to a higher law! Their conscience was like a judge and jury, presiding in the courtroom of their hearts. Conscience is the voice of God in the soul.

The problem with the voice of our conscience, is that we are living in a world and inhabit bodies infected by sin, which can change or damage our conscience, or inner voice. We might compare our conscience to an alarm clock. It's initial design, is to go off when we violate God's moral code. Alarm clocks however can be turned on or off as suits us; they can be turned down so that they no longer disturb us; and of course there is the ever present snooze button! We are all experts at justifying and rationalising our attitudes and behaviour. The fact that God has given us this internal alarm clock, reveals not only that moral agents but that we are accountable to God for our lives. Guilt is a real thing. Our conscience is connected with our senses of guilt. When we fail morally or sin, we can dismiss it, deny it, distort it, or deal with it. Our God given conscience is designed to help us deal with our sin.

A clear conscience is a wonderful thing in the day of accusation. It liberates us from fear and instills courage. Proverb 28:1 says, 'The wicked flee when no man pursueth: but the righteous are as bold as a lion'.

God certainly does not desire us to over-sensitize our conscience with needless, neurotic guilt. We must never forget the grace of God extended to us through the Lord Jesus Christ that promises us forgiveness. The atoning work of Jesus Christ on the cross has freed us from all sin past, present and future. At the same time, God does not want our conscience to be desensitized and defiled. Thank God for your conscience. Make the most of this God given gift. Instead of letting your conscience be your guide, we must make sure our conscience is guided by the Word of God.

Excerpts from The Voice Of Our Conscience
www.gospelweb.net/ronsermons4/TheVoiceOfOurConscience

The Secret Place

My heart is like a house
One day I let the Savior in
And there are many rooms
Where we would visit now and then
But then one day
He saw that door
I knew the day had come too soon
I said, "Jesus I'm not ready
For us to visit in that room

Cause that's a place in my heart
Where even I don't go
I have some things hidden there
I don't want anyone to know"
But He handed me the keys
With tears of love on His face
He said, "I want to make you clean
Let me go in your secret place."

So I opened up the door
And as the two of us walked in
I was so ashamed
His light revealed my hidden sin
But when I think about that room now

I'm not afraid anymore
Cause I know my hidden sin
No longer hides behind that door

That was a place in my heart
Where even I wouldn't go
I had some things hidden there
I didn't want anyone to know
But He handed me the keys
With tears of love on His face
He made me clean
I let Him in my secret place

(Steve Chapman/Careers-BMG Music Pub./Shepherd's Fold Music/Star Song

From the CD "Family Favorites"/Steve and Annie Chapman

EPILOGUE

Place – San Diego, California
Year – 2015

His Decision

His heels clicked against the long sterile corridor and echoed throughout the prison wing. Alan Moses sensed an increasing déjà vu as he walked through a double oak door remembering another double oak door- at New Life Tabernacle back in London. That was seven years ago, he was a broken man then, stunned by the ramifications of his actions agonizing about a decision that could have dire consequences. But hope pushed him forward.

He remembered the day as if it was yesterday. The day that Randy Jacob died. The lie he was living, buried. Buried in a watery grave.

You'll be a new man, Pastor McKenzie had told him. *Old things will pass away and all things will become new.* His deep, resonant, pastoral voice was a comfort to Alan's desperate and weary soul as he went down the steps into the baptismal pool that day. *Alan Moses, upon the confession of your faith, I now baptise you in the name of Jesus Christ for the remission of your sins and ye shall receive the gift of the Holy Ghost.*

Pastor McKenzie then submerged him in the cool water. He remembered his heart racing wildly as the water washed over him and then coming up to the applause of the church. Anton's wife Denise broke into a song '*I Surrender All*' and that's when it happened. An overwhelming peace and an unspeakable joy descended as Alan closed his eyes and lifted his hands in complete surrender. He felt empowered like a drowning victim, swimming to the surface and gulping fresh breaths of air.

He literally felt the weight lift.

Someone touched Him. He could not explain it but he just knew. A knowing in your knower as Anton would say. A praise rose from deep within.

Alan didn't know how long he was in the pool with his arms outstretched in worship. When his eyes finally opened the first face he saw was Jessica, Anton's ten year old daughter. She was grinning from cheek to cheek. '*I'm so excited*' she later told Alan, '*the angels are rejoicing because of you. That's what the Bible says There is joy in heaven when a sinner repents*'.

She'll be seventeen now Alan mused as he walked into a large room accompanied by the prison chaplain and a female guard. Several folding chairs were set up in a loose formation of rows facing the front.

'The reporters are on the way,' the chaplain said, 'Before they arrive Alan, I really want to thank you for being willing to do this interview. Coming forward with your story is an amazing opportunity to reach a lot of people'.

Alan reflected how hard he had prayed about the journey ahead of him. 'I'd do anything to bring your daughter back', he'd sobbed to Gaby's grief stricken parents at the trial. But as the days turned into weeks and weeks became months and the months years her parents had accepted his heartfelt remorse. They were tired of holding on to anger and hatred they said. Alan's personal story of redemption had touched several of his inmates to the point that many were giving their lives to Christ.

Alan Moses felt humbled to think that he could actually make a difference from the gray surroundings in which he found himself in. To reach people with his heartfelt message that there is no pit so deep that God's love is not deeper still.

'NBC wanted to interview this man who had shown such courage and fortitude by voluntarily giving himself up.

ABOUT THE AUTHOR

 I was born in London, grew up in Texas and now reside in the West Midlands with my husband Tony. We are the proud parents of three grown sons who have blessed us with four grandchildren. My husband and I attend New Life Fellowship United Pentecostal church in Bilston, West Midlands where we are both actively involved.

When I am not looking for a story to write, where characters face adversity and overcome with their faith still intact, I'm enjoying the privileged world of grandparenthood, reading and listening to gospel music especially jazz gospel.

I believe there is no pit too deep that Jesus cannot pick you out of.

Wherefore He is able also to save them to the uttermost that come unto God by him, seeing He ever liveth to make intercession for them
Hebrews 7:25

Printed in the United States
By Bookmasters